Joseph Trapani

Gulliver's
Travels

I = Inference

For Kayla, whose travels are just beginning
—N.E.

*To Brianne, Derek, and Benjamin, who help bring many
of my imaginings to life*
—J.W.

Text copyright © 2010 by Nicholas Eliopulos
Illustrations copyright © 2010 by John Walker

All rights reserved.
Published in the United States by Random House Children's Books,
a division of Random House, Inc., New York.

Random House and the colophon are registered trademarks and A Stepping Stone Book and the colophon are trademarks of Random House, Inc.

Visit us on the Web!
www.steppingstonesbooks.com
www.randomhouse.com/kids

Educators and librarians, for a variety of teaching tools, visit us at
www.randomhouse.com/teachers

Library of Congress Cataloging-in-Publication Data
Eliopulos, Nick.
Gulliver's travels / by Jonathan Swift ; adapted by Nick Eliopulos ;
illustrated by John Walker.
p. cm.
"A Stepping Stone Book."
Summary: The voyages of an Englishman carry him to such strange places as Lilliput, where people are six inches tall; Brobdingnag, a land of giants; and a country ruled by horses.
ISBN 978-0-375-86569-5 (pbk.) — ISBN 978-0-375-96569-2 (lib. bdg.)
— ISBN 978-0-375-89819-8 (e-book)
[1. Voyages and travels—Fiction. 2. Fantasy.] I. Walker, John, 1957– ill.
II. Swift, Jonathan, 1667–1745. Gulliver's travels. III. Title.
PZ7.E417Gu 2010   [Fic]—dc22   2009035655

Printed in the United States of America
10 9 8 7 6 5 4 3 2

Gulliver's Travels

by Jonathan Swift
adapted by Nick Eliopulos
illustrated by John Walker

A STEPPING STONE BOOK™
Random House 🏠 New York

Chapter 1

My name is Lemuel Gulliver. I have always wanted to see the world.

From an early age, I did everything I could to get ready for a life of adventure. I studied maps for hours and hours. I learned many languages. I exercised to become as strong as a sailor.

My hard work paid off in the year 1699. The captain of a ship called the *Antelope* hired me. The *Antelope* was sailing to the southern Pacific Ocean, far from my home in England. I said good-bye to my family and began my adventure.

The first six months at sea were tough. But I was happy working on board the ship. Too soon, that happiness was taken away.

We were drifting through a thick mist on a hazy afternoon. It was hard to see. No one noticed a rock sticking out of the water until our ship crashed into it. I was thrown overboard.

I heard men shouting. They scrambled for the lifeboats. But I could not even see the ship through all the fog. My cries for help were lost among the other shouts.

The tide pulled me away from my fellow sailors. To save myself, I had to swim in the direction the ocean pushed me. I only hoped that the rock in the sea meant land was nearby.

Just as I was almost too tired to go on, my feet touched bottom. I walked the rest of the way to land. By then, it was night. Exhausted, I lay down on the grass and fell asleep.

I woke up in the morning to an unhappy surprise. I was unable to stand. In fact, I could not move at all!

Thin, strong strings held my body. My arms and legs were tied to the ground. So was my hair.

I felt something on my leg—something alive. It crossed my stomach and my chest. When it was nearly at my chin, it stopped. I turned my eyes down just enough to see what it was.

It was a man. He was only six inches tall!

In his hands were a tiny bow and

why was a man there.

3

arrow. A moment later, dozens of equally small men joined him. I could hardly believe my eyes.

I roared, and they all ran away. I struggled to stand. My left arm came free of its strings. With a painful tug, I also loosened the strings that held my hair.

That was as far as I got. There was a shrill cry in a language I did not know. Then a hundred little men fired arrows at me. The arrows struck my left hand and stung like needles. Other men tried to stab me in the side with spears. But their weapons could not cut through my leather jacket.

I stopped moving, and the wave of arrows and spears came to an end.

One of the men stepped forward. I could now turn my head enough to see him. He was clearly a leader of this small army. But I could not understand him. He did not understand my words, either.

Luckily, he understood the signs I made with my free hand. I asked for food and drink because I was terribly hungry and thirsty.

The leader barked some orders in a high-pitched voice. Several small ladders were leaned against my side. Men climbed them with baskets of food and barrels of wine. They emptied them into my mouth. It took quite a lot before I was full.

I did not know that the wine had been drugged with a sleeping potion.

When I woke up again, I was tied to a sheet of wood that had twenty-two wheels. It was a cart, pulled by one thousand five hundred horses. Each horse was about four and a half inches tall.

Even with so many horses, it was a slow trip across the countryside. Two days later, we came within view of the city gates. But we did not enter. Instead we stopped at an ancient temple.

The king's blacksmiths met us there. They carried a long chain. It was made of many smaller chains tied together. They locked the chain to my left leg with thirty-six padlocks. Then they looped it through the temple's windows.

Once the chain was in place, the men at last cut the strings that bound me. For the first time in days, I stood up.

When the crowd saw how tall I was, they let out a tiny, amazed roar.

The countryside around the temple looked like a garden to me. The tallest trees were about my height. The farmers' fields were like flower beds.

As I looked around, the emperor of the land of Lilliput came over. He wore simple clothes, but on his head was a helmet of gold and jewels with a feather on top. He held a three-inch sword in his hand.

His voice was high-pitched. But he spoke loudly enough that I could hear him even when I stood. Sadly, I had no idea what he was saying. I spoke to him

He couldn't understand the emperor.

first in English. Then I tried every other language I knew—German, Portuguese, Dutch, Latin, Greek, French, Spanish, and Italian. It was no good.

Although we could not understand each other, the emperor made it clear that he was a kind and generous ruler. He had brought many carts full of food and drink. The people cheered when I lifted the carts to my mouth.

The emperor soon left, but hundreds of little people stayed to watch me. Several soldiers kept the crowd under control. Still, when they were not looking, someone in the crowd shot an arrow at me. The arrow almost hit me in the eye!

To punish the prankster, the soldiers handed him over to me. I decided to play a trick of my own. I grabbed the young man and raised him slowly to my face. I licked my lips. Finally I opened my mouth as if I were going to eat him!

The man cried out in fright. The crowd held its breath. But I laughed and put the man on the ground.

He ran off, never looking back.

Chapter 2

With my leg chained, I could not walk more than two yards from the temple. But I could lay my entire body down inside the building. It was both my home and my prison.

All the nearby villages delivered six cows, forty sheep, and ten carts of bread to my temple each day. Six hundred people served me as butlers, cooks, and maids. They slept in tents just outside my temple. Three hundred tailors were asked to make a suit for me. A hundred women sewed six hundred tiny beds together to make one large bed. And six schoolteachers taught me their language.

Even so, I was a prisoner. As long as the people were afraid of me, I would never be free. So I was on my best behavior.

Sometimes I lay on my back and let men and women dance in my palms. Children played games of hide-and-seek in my hair. Soldiers rode their horses all around me, leaping over my hands and feet.

Months passed, and I asked again and again to have my chain removed. The emperor wanted to set me free. But not everyone agreed.

Skyresh Bolgolam was one of the emperor's most trusted advisers. He argued to keep me locked up.

One day, Skyresh was finally out-voted. But Skyresh added one condition to my freedom. I had to agree to a contract. Skyresh brought the contract to my temple himself. It said:

1. The Man-Mountain shall not leave the country of Lilliput without permission.
2. He shall not enter the capital city unless invited.
3. He shall walk only upon our roads. He will not trample our fields.
4. He shall be careful not to trample our people or horses, either.
5. When a messenger must travel a great distance, that

messenger may ask the
Man-Mountain to carry him.
In those cases, the Man-
Mountain shall carry the
messenger and the horse in
his pocket.

6. He shall be our ally against
   our enemies on the island
   of Blefuscu.

In exchange for his promises,
the Man-Mountain shall
receive a daily allowance of
food. The amount of food will
be enough to keep 1,728
Lilliputians well fed and happy.

I swore to obey these rules. Still,
Skyresh gave me a sour look when my
chain was unlocked. I knew he would

always be an enemy of mine. But at long last, I was free to move about the land!

The next day, I visited the capital city. I easily stepped over its two-foot walls. The people had been told to stay within their homes. They crowded at windows and on rooftops to watch me pass on the way to the palace. How did he enter the palace.

15

the PIIace WAS HUge.

The palace itself was incredible. Its walls were so high that even I could not step over them. With His Majesty's permission, I lay down to look through the windows. There I saw richly decorated rooms. The empress was going about her business. She stuck her hand outside the window so that I could kiss it.

Usually, though, I did not go far from my temple home. Many people came to visit me there. One was a lord of the emperor's court named Reldresal. He had argued with Skyresh on the subject of my freedom. I was always happy to see him. I held him in my palm when we spoke.

One day, Reldresal explained that the emperor wanted my help in Lilliput's war against its island neighbor,

Blefuscu. The fighting between these two empires reached back hundreds of years. It had begun because the men and women of Lilliput believed that anyone who cooked with an egg should crack the egg open on its smaller end. The people of Blefuscu did not agree. They thought an egg should be broken only on its larger end.

I felt each person should choose his or her own way to crack an egg. But I had agreed in the contract to help Lilliput.

Blefuscu had caused Lilliput much trouble with its fleet of ships. I came up with a plan that I hoped would put an end to the bloody war. I asked for a great deal of rope and the strongest iron bars in the empire. I bent the tiny iron bars into hooks. I also braided many ropes together to make long cords. It looked as if I were going fishing.

With these tools, I walked to the northeast coast of Lilliput. I took off my coat and waded into the water. Then I swam the narrow channel until Blefuscu's fleet of ships came into view.

The men on the ships screamed at the sight of me. No one on that side of the channel had ever seen a Man-Mountain. The sailors dove into the water and swam for shore. Their ships were left empty.

I fixed a hook to each of the ships. The people on the beach realized what I was doing. They fired arrow after arrow at me. But I had been smart enough to wear my reading glasses. With my eyes covered, the arrows did me no harm. I swam away, pulling the entire fleet of ships along behind me.

Back in Lilliput, the people cheered my victory. I was a hero. They plucked the arrows from my skin and soothed the cuts with medicine.

The emperor was so pleased that he began making plans to attack Blefuscu. He wanted to become its ruler. But I told him that peace was better. I had stolen the fleet so that Blefuscu would not invade Lilliput. I could not turn around and help Lilliput invade Blefuscu.

Soon after, the two empires signed a peace treaty. They still disagreed about eggs, but their war was over at last.

It was not long before I had a chance to do the emperor another great favor.

One night, the cries of many people at my door woke me. Again and again, they repeated the word "burglum." It was their word for fire!

The crowd begged me to hurry to the palace. The empress's rooms had caught on fire from a candle.

By the light of the moon, I made my way to the palace as quickly as I could without trampling any of the people. Dozens of men and women were throwing buckets of water at the blaze. The buckets were about the size of thimbles. The fire was so big that the water did little good.

Then I had a marvelous idea. I decided to empty my bladder directly on the fire.

Within minutes, the fire was out. The palace was saved!

Chapter 3

Not everyone thought I was a hero. Late one night, Reldresal paid me a surprise visit. This time, he asked to speak to me in private. I sent my servants away and bolted the door. Then I placed the lord on my table.

"Skyresh Bolgolam has been your enemy since you got here," he told me. "Now he hates you even more since you defeated Blefuscu's fleet without his help."

a group of ships

This was unhappy news. But the lord had more to say.

"The empress is against you, too.

She is disgusted by the way you saved the burning palace. Together, she and Skyresh have convinced the emperor that you must be punished."

"Punished!" I said. "How?"

"They argued that you should be shot with poison arrows," Reldresal said. "But since the emperor is a fair and just ruler, he has decided only to blind you. His doctors will put arrows into your eyeballs as you lie on the ground. This will be done in three days. I wanted to warn you."

I thanked the lord. I had not known many kings or emperors in my life. But I could not believe that this punishment was either fair or just.

I had to leave. The next day, I swam again across the channel to Blefuscu.

The emperor and his wife came out to meet me. I lay upon the ground to kiss their hands. I did not tell them I was running away. I only said that I wanted to see their land. Since the war was over, they welcomed me.

For the time being, I was safe. But that night, I slept upon the ground with neither a roof above me nor a bed below me.

Three days later, I was walking along the coast when I saw something out in the water. It looked like an over-turned boat. I pulled off my shoes and waded into the water. It *was* a boat! And it was large enough that I could sit in it!

I swam to the boat and pushed it to the shore. It was hardly damaged at all.

I told the emperor that luck had led

me to this boat. I asked for the help of his most skilled men and women.

Five hundred of the king's people were given the job of making two sails from their strongest cloth. Even so, the cloth had to be folded over many times to be thick enough.

I made ropes and cables by twisting together ten, twenty, or thirty of the biggest ropes they had. I cut down trees to make the ship's masts and oars. For an anchor, I found a great stone on the shore.

In a month, I was ready to leave. I loaded the little sailboat with the meat of a hundred oxen and three hundred sheep, as well as bread and wine.

I also took eight live cows and eight live sheep, with a good bundle of hay to feed them. I wanted to show the tiny animals to my countrymen. I would have brought some people, too, but the emperor would not let me. He said he trusted me. But he had his soldiers check my pockets just in case.

I was at sea for three days before I saw a ship in the distance. I rowed as fast as I could. The wind was working in my favor. Within half an hour, the sailors raised an English flag and fired a gun in the air. They had seen me!

Rescued at last, I felt more joy than I had known in all my time as the Man-Mountain of Lilliput.

Chapter 4

I stayed at home for only two months. Then I set out on my next trip.

We had good winds behind us all the way down the western coast of Africa and around the Cape of Good Hope. But as we passed Madagascar, the sea and the sky became eerily calm. There was no wind at all. The quiet made me happy, but the captain knew it meant a storm was coming.

The storm hit the very next day. The waves were large. The wind was fierce. We tore down the sails so that the boat would not be blown over. It took several sailors working together to steer against the angry sea.

When the storm passed, we found it had blown us far off course. Our ship was in fine shape. We had plenty of food. The crew was all in good health. But we were lost and running out of drinking water.

For days, we drank as little water as possible. I felt a great rush of relief when a voice cried out from our ship's crow's nest. Our lookout had spotted land!

We cast anchor near the shore. Then our captain sent a dozen men in a rowboat to get freshwater. I went with them.

On the shore, we split up. I wandered alone, but I found no stream or river. When I returned to the beach, my fellow sailors were in the rowboat, why was it covered with sharp rocks

rowing for our ship as if their lives depended on it. They were leaving me behind!

I was going to shout out, but I saw something that froze me in my tracks. A giant man was chasing them through the water!

The giant moved slowly, as if the sea bottom was covered with sharp rocks. His enormous arms reached out, but the sailors had a head start. The boat was a safe distance away.

I stayed no longer. I ran as fast as I could in the other direction, up a hill and down a very wide dirt road. The plants on either side of the road towered above me. The grass was twenty feet high. The corn was at least twice as tall as the grass. And the trees were so tall

everything was big

I think he will hide somewhere

that I could not even guess their height.

I spotted a second giant on the road ahead of me. He was as tall as a great church steeple. He had not seen me yet, but he was walking my way. His steps were so large that he would reach me in moments.

Struck with fear, I ran into the massive cornfield beside the road. To my bad luck, the giant moved in the same direction. And he was not alone. He called out in a voice so loud that I thought it was thunder. The next moment, seven more giants came into view.

They entered the cornfield with huge blades in their hands. I realized to my horror that it was harvest season. The giants swung their deadly tools,

why was he tried to get away

cutting down stalk after stalk of corn.

I tried to get away, but it was difficult to squeeze between the stalks. It was like moving through an overgrown forest.

In front of me, the corn had been crushed to the ground by rain or wind. The fallen stalks were woven together so tightly that it was impossible to pass between them. It was a dead end!

One of the monsters came near. With his next step, I would be either squashed to death by his foot or cut in two with his blade. So I screamed as loudly as fear could make me.

The huge creature stopped. He looked at the ground for some time before he even saw me. Then he watched me carefully. It was as if I were a cornered animal that might bite him.

I think he will be mad.

Finally he reached down, grasped me between his finger and thumb, and brought me close to his face.

He held me sixty feet above the ground. I decided it was better not to struggle. Instead I begged for his mercy. I think he understood, for he did not hurt me. He ran back to the main path and brought me to the giant with the voice like thunder.

The astonished farmer took me in his hand. He used a piece of straw to poke at my clothes. He blew my hair to get a better view of my face. At last he put me on the ground, placing me on all fours as if I were an animal.

Right away I stood up. I bowed, and lifting my chin, I spoke as loudly as I could. "Good afternoon, kind farmer," I said.

The farmer clearly did not understand my words. He tried speaking to me, but I could not understand him, either. The loudness of his voice hurt my ears.

After he sent his workers back to the field, he carried me to his house on his gigantic handkerchief. At the sight of me, his wife leaped into a chair and screamed! But I bowed my head to her. It was the polite thing to do.

Surely impressed by my manners, the farmer's wife became more curious than afraid. She set the table for lunch and had the farmer place me near her enormous plate of food. The table was thirty feet above the floor, so I sat as far as I could from the edge.

The wife cut a small bit of meat from her plate. She brushed some crumbs from her bread, and she put this food in front of me. I made a low bow, took out my fork from my pocket, and ate. I drank cider from a thimble. I needed both hands to lift it.

After lunch, the farmer went back outside. Seeing me yawn, the farmer's wife put me on her bed. She covered me with a handkerchief as large and as tough as the sail of a ship. I fell asleep instantly.

I woke up with the sense that I was in danger. And indeed I was. Two rats, as big as wolves, were crawling up the curtains. They crept from the curtains to the bed, sniffing the entire time. They were following my scent!

There was nowhere for me to run. The bed was eight yards from the floor. Even if I could get down, I could never open the bedroom door. I had to fight.

I drew my sword just as the first rat attacked. It opened its savage mouth. But I was quick and cut its stomach open with my sword. It fell at my feet.

The second rat turned and ran away. I slashed it in the back as it fled.

After a few minutes, the farmer's wife came into the room. She saw I was covered in blood, and scooped me up in her hands. I pointed to the dead rat and smiled so that she would know I had not been hurt. But it was clear to both of us that this land held many dangers for me.

He might get hurt again.

Chapter 5

In the following weeks, the farmer's nine-year-old daughter took care of me. She was small for her age, standing only forty feet tall. But she was very helpful. She made a bed out of a doll's cradle. At night, she placed this bed on a shelf that no rats could reach. She sewed new outfits for me and washed my clothes in the sink when they were dirty.

She also helped me learn her language. I would point to an object, and she would tell me the word for it.

The girl gave me a new name—Grildrig. It meant "small person." I called her Glumdalclitch, or "little nurse."

Meanwhile, the farmer came up with a plan to make money. We were going to travel to the far-off capital city and stop at towns along the way. At each town, the farmer would show me to curious strangers. A little man was already an unusual sight. The fact that I could speak their language made me even more interesting. To the giants, it was as if a mouse had learned to talk.

The farmer and Glumdalclitch rode on horseback. The girl sat behind her father, while I sat in a box on her lap. She had kindly lined the box with a quilt. She had also cut holes in the lid to let air in.

In the first town, the farmer rented a

room at an inn. There he hired a town crier. This boy ran throughout the town, announcing the strange creature at the inn. "You have to see it to believe it!" he shouted.

Soon the people came to the inn. They paid the farmer and entered our room.

I stood on a table. My little nurse sat on a stool nearby and gave me instructions. I walked where she directed. I answered the questions that she asked as loudly as I could. I swung my sword. I threw a piece of straw as if it were a javelin.

The crowd cheered my many talents. At first I was happy to bring them such joy. But by the end of the day, I was falling over with exhaustion.

The next morning, we were on the

road again. We visited a new town every day for weeks. I saw much of the kingdom, which they called Brobdingnag. My skill with their language became better each day. But my body grew weak from traveling and performing.

Glumdalclitch often took me out of my box as we rode. She wanted me to enjoy the fresh air. But she always kept me safe on a leash.

When we finally got to the capital city, we rented a room on the main street. Many people lived in the capital, so I performed several days in a row.

One day, a special visitor was in the crowd. The queen of Brobdingnag had heard of me. She had sent her messenger to invite us to the palace.

I performed all of my best tricks for

the queen. Her Majesty was delighted. After my show was done, she let me kiss her pinkie finger. I hugged it with both arms and put the tip of it to my lips.

We spoke for a short time. She was curious about where I had come from. After I answered many questions, she had one final thing to ask me.

"Would you like to live here in the palace?" she asked.

In truth, I liked the idea very much. I was tired from my life on the road. But I was not free to choose. I bowed and answered, "I would happily spend my life here, but I belong to my master, the farmer."

The queen turned to the farmer. "Would you sell him for a good price?" she asked.

The farmer was a greedy man. He sold me to the queen for one thousand pieces of gold.

As the farmer gathered his gold, I asked the queen for a favor. Could Glumdalclitch stay by my side? She had always treated me with kindness, and I needed a nurse to take care of me.

Her Majesty agreed. The farmer also agreed, knowing his daughter would live well in the palace. The girl was full of joy.

The queen took me in her hand and carried me to meet the king. At first he thought I was a rodent. Then he said I must be a windup toy. But when I spoke, he could not hide his surprise. He welcomed me to his palace.

Chapter 6

On my first day in the palace, the queen hired a very skilled carpenter. He crafted a box to be my bedroom. It was a marvel! It had a door and windows, a table and chairs, and closets. The ceiling was on hinges. Glumdalclitch lifted it open to make my tiny bed each day and tuck me in each night. I could open a small hatch in the ceiling for fresh air.

There was an iron ring on top of the box so that Glumdalclitch could carry it. Inside, my room was quilted on all sides. If I fell during travel, I would not get hurt.

Other inventions were all my own. On one occasion, I watched a barber shave the king's face. As I saw the stubble fall to the ground, I had an idea.

I gathered about fifty of the short, strong hairs. Next I carved a piece of wood and poked holes into it with Glumdalclitch's smallest needle. I fit the king's hairs into the holes. In this way, I made a perfect comb for my own hair.

I enjoyed my new life. But even at the palace, there was much to fear. The land was overrun with flies during the summer. They were small enough that they did not bother the queen or her subjects. But to me, they were the size of songbirds.

They constantly buzzed around me as I ate. Sometimes they landed on my food and made a mess on it. Other times they landed on my head. I could see and feel the slime on their feet.

And I once had to defend myself against a more dangerous insect. Glumdalclitch had set my box on an open windowsill. I was sitting at my table, eating breakfast and enjoying the summer breeze. Suddenly, twenty wasps flew in through my window.

Some of them seized my breakfast, carrying it away. Others flew around my head. Their stingers terrified me.

I drew my sword and attacked. Four wasps fell to my blade. The rest escaped. I shut the window. Then, with my sword, I cut the stingers from the dead wasps' bodies. The stingers were each an inch and a half long and sharp as needles.

Bugs were not nature's only danger.
One day, I was walking through the
queen's garden when the sky grew dark.
A sudden shower of hail fell to the
ground. I tucked my legs beneath me and

covered my head with my hands. The hail struck my body like hundreds of tennis balls. Afterward I was so bruised that I could not leave my bed for a week.

A more dangerous accident happened in the same garden when a small white dog caught my scent. It took me in its mouth and ran straight to its master, the gardener. Wagging its tail, the dog set me on the ground as if playing a game of fetch. The poor gardener feared I was dead, but after I caught my breath, I told him I was fine.

But the greatest danger I ever faced was from a monkey. It came through Glumdalclitch's bedroom window. The animal bounced around, pulling objects from shelves and tabletops. It made a mess of the room.

At last it came to my box. It peeked through the windows and the door. I hid in the corner. But the monkey saw me. It reached through the door, grabbing at me with its paw. I danced around to avoid it. My heart raced, and I grew short of breath. Finally it caught hold of my coat and dragged me out the door.

The strange animal cradled me in its arms as if I were its baby. I lay still. I did not know what else to do.

Just then, Glumdalclitch entered the room and screamed in surprise. The monkey leaped to the open window. Holding me tightly, it used its three other paws to climb to the roof.

From that great and terrifying height, I saw a crowd form below. Some people ran for ladders. Others threw rocks. But that only made me more afraid. What if the tremendous rocks hit me? What if the monkey fell, with me still in its grasp?

Several men began climbing the ladders. The monkey saw them coming. It dropped me upon the roof and sped off, chattering as it went.

I lay flat on the roof tile for some time. I was five hundred yards from the ground. A gust of wind could have knocked me right over the edge. But a stable boy reached me before that happened. He took me up in his hands, placed me in his pocket, and climbed back down the ladder.

Chapter 7

I missed my freedom. I wanted to walk streets and fields without worrying that I would be trampled to death or stolen away by some animal.

Such things were on my mind when I rode with Glumdalclitch and the royal family to the coast. They had a second palace near the ocean. The seaside was beautiful. But it was too dangerous for me to walk along the shore on my own.

Still, I wanted to see the ocean and feel the sea air. Glumdalclitch was in bed with a cold. So instead the stable boy who had rescued me from the monkey offered to take me to the beach.

My poor nurse hated to let me out of her sight. She made the boy promise to be careful with me. It was almost as if she knew something bad would happen.

The stable boy carried me in my box to the rocky coast. I sat upon my roof and watched the waves break as the boy looked for birds' eggs among the rocks. After a while, I grew tired. I went inside, closing the door behind me to keep out the chill, and lay down for a nap.

A sudden jolt woke me up. It felt as though someone had grabbed the ring on top of my box. But I could not see anyone through the windows.

The box rose high into the air. Then it moved swiftly forward. All I saw from the windows were clouds and sky.

I was flying!

I called for help, but it was hopeless. I grew quiet and heard a noise coming from the other side of my ceiling. It sounded like the flapping of giant wings. I knew that some great bird had my box in its grasp.

Suddenly, my box was tossed about like a leaf in the wind. The wings were not just flapping now. They were slapping other wings. The first bird was under attack from a second bird!

The box began to fall. I gripped the table, which was nailed to the floor. I nearly lost my stomach as I dropped for a full minute at a terrible speed.

There was a sound like a waterfall, and all went dark.

Slowly, the box rose. Light returned

to the windows. I had fallen into the sea.
I could see sky at the tops of my windows and water at the bottoms.

Hours passed. I paced in fear. A
crack in a single window would mean
certain death. And even if the windows
did not break, I would be dead of cold or
hunger within days. The blind dropped
sulliven into the ocean.
his box is protecting him.

While in this unhappy state, I heard a scraping noise on the windowless side of my box. Soon after, I felt the box being pulled through the sea. The waves rose and fell against my windows.

I stood on my chair and threw open the hatch in the ceiling. It was too small to climb through. I called for help in every language I knew.

To my great joy, I heard a voice call out in English. "Is there someone in there?" it asked.

"I am an Englishman, lost at sea!" I cried. "Can you get me out of here?"

"Do not worry, friend," the voice answered. "You are safe now. We have hooked your prison to our ship. We will bring a saw so that we can cut you out of there."

"Why not just lift the lid?" I asked. When no answer came, I explained, "You could just stick your finger in the hole and lift."

There was laughter. I had assumed a giant was outside. But actually I was speaking to a man of my own size.

A larger hole was sawed into the ceiling. A ladder dropped down. I climbed out and onto the deck of a ship.

The sailors were all amazed to have found me in a floating house. They asked a thousand questions. But I could only stare at them and laugh.

I laughed because I was used to seeing giants. And I had forgotten how *small* people really are.

Chapter 8

My bad luck at sea did not kill my desire *[dreams/wish]* to see the world. So I spent only a few months at home before getting a job on a new ship, the *Hopewell*.

Two weeks into our voyage to the East Indies, we saw two pirate ships in the distance. We tried to outrun them, but their ships were faster. They pulled up right beside us. Dozens of pirates boarded our boat.

We did not fight. We knew we could not win. They tied us up and searched our cargo. After they took what they wanted, they destroyed everything else.

The pirates planned to force the men of the *Hopewell* to work on their ships. I could not bear to see such good men become prisoners. I said so very loudly and with much emotion. After this, the pirate captains decided I was a trouble-maker. They did not want me on their ships.

I was put into a small canoe with a sail, paddles, and four days' worth of food and water. Then I was set adrift. My chance of finding rescue out on the vast blue sea was small.

I rowed a good distance away from the pirates before taking out my spy-glass. Looking through it, I spotted an island to the southeast. I reached it just before nightfall.

The land was rocky and treeless. But

I built a fire using dry seaweed. I cooked and ate a small dinner. Exhausted by hours of rowing, I soon fell asleep.

I woke feeling anxious. I could not survive long in such a barren place. The sun was frightfully hot in the day, with no trees for shade. The sky had no clouds. But as I walked among the rocks, suddenly a deep shade fell over me. It was as if I stood under a mountain.

I turned to see what had blocked the sun. It was not a mountain. It was not a cloud or a tree. It was an island.

A flying island.

The island was huge, with sloping green hills. Its bottom half was a jagged hunk of rock. It floated a mile above the sea, moving slowly past my own island.

Through my spyglass, I saw people.

He will try to get up to the island.

They walked along balconies and stair-cases that wrapped around the outside of the island. Some of them were fishing in the ocean—with fishing line a mile long!

This was my best chance for rescue. I waved my handkerchief and shouted at the top of my voice.

A crowd gathered on the balcony closest to me. It was clear that they had seen me. They pointed. Some of them ran upstairs to the top of the island.

In a matter of minutes, the island slowed to a stop. It hovered in the air, unmoving. Then it changed direction. Soon it was directly over my head.

A chain was let down from the lowest balcony. It had a seat attached to it, like a swing. I sat down. Holding the chain tightly, I was pulled up into the sky.

On the island, I was met by two men. They were dressed unlike anyone I had ever seen. Their clothing was decorated with suns, moons, and stars, as well as fiddles, flutes, harps, trumpets, and guitars. There were even musical instruments we do not have in Europe.

But their clothing was not the strangest thing about these men. One of them had a faraway look in his eyes, as if he was daydreaming. The other held in his hand a small sack, like a coin purse. Every so often, he hit the first man in the face with it.

I later learned that these sacks, filled with pebbles or dried peas, were called flaps. Men and women who used them were called flappers.

I looked around. Most of the people

on the island had the same blank look as the first man. They did not notice me.

The two men made signs that I should follow them up the stairs. But it was a slow journey. The first man often forgot where we were going. He would walk off in the wrong direction or stop moving altogether. Each time, the flapper struck him. Then the man walked for a time in the right direction.

At long last, we got to the palace and stood before the king. Deep in thought, he sat at a table covered with spheres and globes and mathematical tools. We waited a full hour before he finally noticed we were there!

One young flapper stood on the king's right. Another stood on his left. The first flapper struck the king on his

the flappers are strange

64

mouth, and the second struck him on his ear. Only then did the king speak to me, in a language I did not know.

The flapper I had come in with slapped my ear with his flap. At last I understood the purpose of all this hitting. The people of the flying island were too smart for their own good. They spent so much time thinking that they forgot to see what was right in front of them.

The flappers had to remind them. A flap to the eye meant "look." A flap to the ear meant "listen." And a flap to the mouth meant "speak."

I waved the flapper away. I did not need a reminder to listen when a king spoke to me. But I could not understand the king anyway. I would have to learn yet another language.

The king was kind enough to give me a room and a private teacher. The first thing I learned was the name of the island—Laputa.

The next morning, a tailor came to make me clothing in the style of Laputa. He did not use a ruler to figure out my size. Instead he used a complex math formula.

Sadly, though, the tailor made a mistake in his calculations. My clothes ended up far too big. But such mistakes were common in Laputa. Very few people had clothes that fit well.

The people of Laputa were even worse at building things. They all drew beautiful blueprints. But the walls of their homes sloped. The roofs did not quite fit. Rain and wind came through the gaps.

Even their music was not very pleasant. Large groups played their instruments for hours without a break. My tutor told me the music was brilliant. But it gave me a headache.

Luckily, their language was not too hard to learn. It was very concerned with math and music. To tell someone he had a beautiful baby, I would say, "Your child looks as pleasant as a triangle." To compliment a chef, I would say, "Your food tastes like a beautiful symphony."

The people rarely made time for such talk. When they did speak, they did not say much I cared to hear. Every one of them was obsessed with the end of the world. They had calculated that one day the sun would grow large enough to swallow the earth. But no one agreed when it would happen. Some thought it would be in a few days. Others thought it would happen in a million years.

They were so worried about this that they never even said "hello" or "good morning." Instead they greeted friends by asking, "Does the sun look healthy to you?"

Talking to such strange people did not interest me. I spent a lot of time looking out to sea as the island floated east. I learned that Laputa was part of a kingdom of islands. But it was the only flying island. It traveled back and forth, passing every town in the king's control. When it moved into position above a town, the people below sent up gifts.

They tied the presents to ropes hung from Laputa's balconies.

If any town rebelled, the king struck back. The flying island could block the sun and the rain, causing a town's crops to die. The people of Laputa sometimes hurled rocks down at the people below. Worst of all, the entire island could be dropped to the ground to crush a town to dust.

A cave at the very center of the island held Laputa's secret—the lodestone. This large, strongly magnetic rock was fixed to the cave walls by a rod. The stone could be spun on this rod, like a wheel on an axle. And it was the reason Laputa could fly.

As with any magnet, one end of the lodestone had a positive charge. The other end was negative. So when the stone faced one direction, the entire island was attracted to the surface of the earth. If the stone was spun around, the island was repelled by the earth.

Scientists in the cave turned the lodestone as the king directed. Their job was important. But I think the flappers had an even more important task. They had to make sure the scientists paid attention to what they were doing!

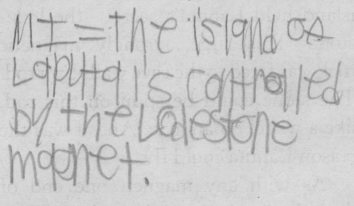
MI = the island of Laputa is controlled by the Lodestone magnet.

Chapter 9

After a while, Laputa eased to a stop above the city of Lagado. I said my farewells. I had seen enough of the people of Laputa. From Lagado, I could make my way home.

But first, I wanted to visit the great academy of Lagado. It was here that the king found the scientists to work in his cave.

The academy was made up of many buildings. I walked from room to room and met hundreds of scientists. But most of their experiments left me scratching my head.

Q = I think he will get back home.

In the first lab, I found a man whose hands and face were covered in soot. His beard was scorched. He had spent eight years trying to pull sunbeams out of cucumbers. He explained that a cucumber takes in sunlight to grow. So we should be able to take the sunlight back again. He figured a cucumber could give back light and heat in even the coldest winters.

In another room was a group of blind scientists. Their job was to mix colors for painters. They believed they could tell colors apart by smell and touch. But to my untrained eye, all their mixtures seemed brown.

Next door, cobwebs covered the walls and ceiling. An old man stood in the one space free of webs. He explained that people relied too much on silk-worms for clothing. Instead, he argued, we should make our clothes from cob-webs. He showed me a handful of color-ful flies. He had dyed the flies and fed them to spiders. He hoped that the col-ored food would lead to colored webs.

"If that works," he said, "I just have to figure out how to make the webs stronger. They break so easily, you know!"

Most of these great men had stu-dents of their own. One wrote all his lessons on crackers, using ink made of medicine. Students swallowed these crackers on an empty stomach. As the cracker was digested, the ink would take the lesson directly to their brains.

It was not clear whether this worked.

The crackers tasted so bad that most students spit them out when the teacher was not looking.

I saw many amazing things at the academy of Lagado. But I heard whispers of an even more amazing place—Glubbdubdrib. A governor ruled this nearby island. He was supposed to be a powerful sorcerer.

I crossed the channel to Glubbdubdrib on a ship. Once there, I learned that the governor had agreed to meet me. He had never met anyone from England. And I had never met a sorcerer!

A wall of twenty-foot stones circled his palace. As I walked through the great wall's gate, I passed two rows of guards. The guards' weapons and uniforms seemed strangely old-fashioned.

Something about them made my skin crawl.

The governor invited me to sit at the foot of his throne. He asked me to tell him about my travels. But before I could begin, he held up his hand.

"I do not want us to be interrupted," he explained. Then he snapped his fingers, and every servant in the room vanished into thin air!

I was quite frightened. The governor promised that I was in no danger. He went on to explain that he could call forth the ghost of any person who had ever lived. Everyone who worked in his palace, from the guards to the chefs, was a ghost.

The governor made me a most unusual offer. He would call forth the ghost of any person from history. The choice was mine.

I asked to meet Alexander the Great.

The governor waved his finger, and Alexander appeared before us in full armor. I had long admired the commander. His travels were even greater than my own.

I had read once that a traitor had poisoned him. I told him I was sad that he had died that way. But the great hero said he had not been poisoned. He had died of a fever.

Many poisons can cause a deadly fever, I pointed out. But the noble ghost explained that his fever had not been caused by poison. It had been caused by drinking too much wine. So he had only himself to blame for his death.

Learning the truth did not make me any happier.

I left Glubbdubdrib soon after that and found a boat that could take me to Japan. In Japan, I joined the crew of a Dutch ship on its way back to Amsterdam. After many months away from Europe, I was on my way home.

Chapter 10

I stayed at home five months. After that, I became the captain of a merchant ship called the *Adventurer*.

From the beginning, it was a difficult trip. While crossing the Atlantic, several of my men died of sickness. The rest blamed me. Early one morning, sailors rushed into my cabin. It was a mutiny! They threatened to throw me overboard if I fought them. They chained my leg to the bed, and a guard stayed at my door.

Weeks passed. One morning, I was told to dress in my best suit of clothes.

The sailors forced me into a boat and rowed it to a beach.

I had been in my cabin all this time, so I had no idea where we were. The sailors claimed not to know, either. They rowed away, leaving me alone in an unknown country.

I walked away from the coast and into a green land of trees, grasses, and oats. After a while, I saw some animals in the distance. I ducked behind a bush to watch them.

Their heads were covered with hair. Half of them had beards like goats and hair on their chests. But the rest of their bodies were hairless. They had no tails. Many of the beasts stood on their hind feet. Others sat in trees, for they had claws sharp enough to help them climb.

They were the ugliest animals I had ever seen. I turned away and walked along the road in the other direction. But I did not get far before one of the creatures stood in my path.

The creature raised its front paw at me. Not sure what it meant to do, I slapped its paw away.

The beast jumped back and roared. To my horror, a herd of forty of the beasts came out of the woods. They howled at me. They made ugly faces.

I backed up against a tree. I was trapped.

All of a sudden, the creatures gasped in fear. They ran away as fast as they could. I turned to see a gray horse coming up the path. I guessed that my attackers had some reason to fear it.

The horse recoiled a little when it saw me. It studied my face. Then its eyes wandered to my hands and feet. It walked around me several times.

I decided to pet the animal. I slowly raised my hand. But the horse shook its head. It pushed my hand away with its hoof and neighed three or four times. Each neigh sounded different from the other. It sounded as if the horse was speaking to itself in some strange language.

Before long, a brown horse came up to us. The two animals struck their right hoofs together and neighed, as if they were saying hello. They walked back and forth, like two people talking about something. But they kept their eyes on me the whole time.

I was amazed to see such behavior. If the animals of this land were so smart, the humans who owned them must be geniuses! very smart person

The gray horse rubbed my vest with his right forehoof. The brown horse poked at my coat. They both seemed confused by my shoes and socks. They felt them with their hoofs and neighed back and forth.

Finally I decided to speak.

"Gentlemen, are you magicians who have changed your shapes?" I asked. "If so, I hope that you are powerful enough to understand my language. I am a poor Englishman, stranded here in your land. I beg one of you, let me ride on your back. Take me to some village, where I can find rest and shelter."

Mr Gulliver wants rest and shelter.

They neighed to each other even more after that. It was clear they were having a serious talk. One word I could make out was "Yahoo." They said it again and again.

As soon as they were silent, I said it back to them: "Yahoo."

Both horses were clearly surprised. The gray horse repeated the word twice. He was teaching me the right way to say it. I said the word again and again. Each time, I got a little better with the accent.

The brown horse then spoke another word, "Houyhnhnm." It was much harder to say. But I did well enough, since they seemed impressed. *liked him*

After a bit more neighing, the horses said farewell. The gray horse moved his head to show me that he wanted me to come with him. I decided to follow him, at least until I found some people.

Whenever I slowed down, the horse cried, "Hhuun-hhuun." I guessed that meant "come on." I tried to make him understand that my legs were tired. But he did not offer to let me ride him.

After three miles, we came to a long building. It was made of logs stuck in the ground. The roof was low and covered with straw.

The horse led me inside. I straightened my jacket and prepared to meet the people of the land. But no people were inside. Instead there were more horses—a mare and two foals. They sat on their haunches upon mats of straw. The room was large, with a smooth clay floor.

Q = Where are the people,
Is this real,

I pinched myself to see if I was dreaming. Were the horses the masters of this house?

The mare rose from her mat and looked me over. She stayed between me and the younger horses as she neighed with the gray horse. I heard the word "Yahoo" again. I was still not sure what it meant.

The gray horse walked out a back door to a courtyard. He said to me, "Hhuun-hhuun." So I followed.

Across the courtyard was another building. Inside were three of those beastly creatures. Ropes around their necks tied them to a post. They held their food—roots and meat—between the claws of their forefeet. They tore at it with their teeth.

"Yahoo," said the horse.

At that moment, I realized something horrible. "Yahoo" was their word for these beasts. And the beasts were actually humans!

The gray horse looked back and forth between me and the Yahoos. He was trying to decide whether we were the same type of animal. I saw only two differences. My nails were trimmed and my face was shaved.

But the horse saw other differences. He had never seen clothing before. To him, my body seemed different from my neck to the tips of my toes.

The horse picked up a root between his hoof and foreleg. He handed it to me, but it was not a kind I knew. Instead of eating it, I handed it back to him. He offered me some of the Yahoos' meat. It smelled so bad that I turned my head away. Next he offered hay, but I shook my head no.

The horse brought his hoof to his mouth. He wanted to know what I would eat.

I turned and pointed to a cow in the field. Then I made movements as if I were milking her.

The horse neighed. He led me inside to a room with jars of fresh milk. I nodded my head and drank.

Soon the family sat down to dinner. The horses again sat on their haunches upon mats of straw. In front of them were four troughs arranged in a square. Each horse had his or her own stack of hay and oats boiled in milk.

They spoke throughout the meal. The foals were very well behaved. And the adults seemed very cheerful.

When dinner was over, the father horse took me aside. By signs he showed that he was worried that I had not eaten anything.

I had an idea. I asked for oats, which they called "hlunnh." I rubbed the oats until the husks came off, and I ground the grain between two stones. Then I added water to make a doughy paste. Toasted in the fire, the paste made a type of bread.

When it grew late, the gray horse led me outside to a shed. I lay down to sleep in the hay.

Chapter 11

For months, I worked very hard to learn the language of the Houyhnhnms. The gray horse was a patient teacher. I called him master.

It was easy to learn the words for things by pointing to every object I saw. The difficult part was the accent. They spoke their words through the nose and the throat in an unusual way.

Many Houyhnhnms came to visit my master to talk with me. They did not believe I was a Yahoo, because my body looked so different. I did not explain that my clothes were not a part of my body. However, my master soon learned the truth.

Every night, after the family had gone to bed, I took off my clothing to use as a blanket. One morning, I slept later than I meant to. My master found me asleep on my bed of hay. I woke up when he whinnied in surprise.

I had no choice but to explain my clothing and shoes. My master found it all very strange. He picked up my clothing in his hoof. He studied each piece. Then he walked around me many times.

"You really are a Yahoo after all," he said.

I was sad to hear him say that. But my master invited me to sit inside by the fire. He asked me to explain where I was from.

"I came from a faraway country," I told him. "I traveled here with fifty others of my kind. We crossed the sea in a great hollow vessel made of wood."

I took my handkerchief and showed

him how a sail could catch the wind.

"But who made this ship?" he asked. "And how is it possible that your Houyhnhnms would trust Yahoos to take care of it?"

"We made this ship ourselves," I told him. "And if I ever return home, no one will believe that I found a place where Houyhnhnms are the masters and Yahoos are the beasts. In England, the opposite is true."

"What are the Houyhnhnms in your country like?" he asked.

"In the summer, they graze in the fields," I answered. "In the winter, they are kept inside with hay and oats. Yahoos rub their skins smooth, comb their manes, and serve them food."

"Ah," he said. "Now I understand.

The Yahoos *think* that they are in charge. But really they are servants to the Houyhnhnms."

"I wish you were right," I said. "We call our Houyhnhnms 'horses.' They are the most beautiful animals we know. They are strong and fast. Horses owned by good people are treated with much care. But when the horses get old or sick, they are sold. They work hard in our fields until they die."

Tears filled my eyes. Suddenly, this all seemed unfair.

I told him how horses are ridden by Yahoos. I explained the use of a bridle, a saddle, a spur, and a whip. I described the heavy carts that horses pull.

My master was shocked. He whinnied. Then he sat in silence.

He said at last, "I find this very upsetting. How could there be a country where Yahoos are in charge of anything? Your eyes point to the front so that you cannot see to the side without turning your head. Your face is so flat that you cannot eat without using your forepaws. You walk on only two legs. Your whole body is so sensitive to the cold that you must cover it up each day."

"I agree with you, my master," I said. "Yahoos are truly a ridiculous animal."

And as I said it, I knew it was true.

Chapter 12

I was happier with the Houyhnhnms than I had ever been in England. So I made an important decision. I would never go back.

My master let me build a one-room shack on his land. I made it the same way the Houyhnhnms make all their buildings. First I found several fallen trees and cut them apart with a sharp stone. Then I shaped the lumber into stakes and drove them into the ground. I wove straw back and forth in the gaps between the stakes.

Several Houyhnhnms helped me.

They used axes and hammers made of stone. They gripped the tools between their hoofs and forelegs.

At other times, I saw them use their hoofs to milk cows and sculpt bowls from clay.

The Houyhnhnms were skilled in many ways. Their poetry was the best I had ever heard. Most of their poems were about friendship. Several poems praised the winners of races and other physical activities.

I ate bread and drank milk every day. I also made butter out of milk, and I found honey. Butter and honey greatly improved the taste of my bread.

Many herbs grew in the land, and I used them for salads. And if I had a craving for meat, I caught a bird or a rabbit using Yahoo hair as a snare.

When my clothes were worn to rags, I made new clothing with the skin of rabbits. I soled my shoes with wood.

One thing I had no use for was a lock for my door. There were no robbers or murderers in Houyhnhnmland. There were no bullies, liars, or cheaters. The Houyhnhnms did not even have words for such things. The only way to say that something was evil or bad was to use the word "Yahoo." So a stone that cuts your foot is "whnaholm Yahoo." Bad weather is "ynlhmndwihlma Yahoo."

My reflection in a lake or in a trough of water reminded me that I had the shape of a Yahoo. But I felt more and more as if I had the soul of a horse. I thought I would live happily among the

Houyhnhnms for the rest of my life. Sadly, I was wrong.

My master called for me early one morning. I could tell right away that he had bad news.

He had been to a meeting. Many Houyhnhnms had told him they did not like him treating a Yahoo like a member of his family. They said it was unnatural. Either I should live with other Yahoos in the wild, or I should be forced to leave the land.

But the first option made some Houyhnhnms nervous. They feared that I could teach the other Yahoos tricks that would make them more dangerous. I had told my master and his neighbors about England. And they had learned for the first time of the frightening Yahoo invention called war.

I was given two months to leave Houyhnhnmland. Full of despair, I fainted at my master's feet.

But there was nothing I could do to fight this cruel fate. I set to work building a boat. In six weeks, I had finished a long canoe. It had paddles of oak and a sail made of the skins of Yahoos. I loaded the boat with food and drink. The time had come to leave my new home.

Battling tears, I walked to the shore with my master and his family. Many of our neighbors had gathered on the beach. I said good-bye to each, saving my master for last. I was going to kneel to kiss his hoof. But he was kind enough to lift his hoof gently to my mouth. I kissed it. My tears flowed freely now.

"Take care of thyself, gentle Yahoo," he said. It sounded like "Hnuy illa nyha, majah Yahoo."

I got into my canoe and pushed off from shore.

My plan was to find a deserted island to spend the rest of my days alone. I wanted only to live in peace and daydream about the greatness of the Houyhnhnms.

After a day of sailing, I found land. I gathered some shellfish on the shore. But if there were any Yahoos nearby, they would see a fire. So I ate my food raw. I camped out on the beach and drank water from a nearby stream.

Three days later, I saw a sail on the water. I watched as it slowly grew larger.

I was sure the boat was coming my way. I ran inland and hid behind a rock.

It was a mistake to hide so near the stream. Several sailors came ashore looking for freshwater. When they found it, they also found me. They stared at my coat made of skins and my wooden-soled shoes. One of them asked me who I was. He spoke in Portuguese.

I answered that I was just a poor Yahoo. I had been banished from the Houyhnhnms.

They laughed at me. I spoke Portuguese well, but the words sounded like I was neighing.

I tried to leave, and they stopped me. They asked one question after another. When they learned that I was from England, they insisted that I come back to their ship. They wanted to take me home. They did not understand when I told them that my true home was lost to me.

I fell to my knees. Again and again, I said that I would not go. But they dragged me all the way to shore. They heaved me into their boat and rowed me to their ship.

The captain's name was Don Pedro. He said many kind things. Indeed, it surprised me to hear a Yahoo speak so politely. But I stayed silent. The smell of him and his men made me want to faint.

I was given a cabin, which I rarely left. I avoided the crew. I refused to dress in their clothing. The months passed slowly.

When I arrived home, the members

of my family all cried for joy. Each of them reached out, grasping at me for a hug. I drew back. I was reminded of my very first meeting with the savage Yahoos of Houyhnhnmland.

Slowly, I have grown used to the Yahoos in my family. I can finally eat in the same room as them, though I must plug my nose with sprigs of lavender. Sometimes I have short talks with them. But they know never to touch me.

I spend most of my time in the stable, where I keep two young horses. I talk with them at least four hours a day, and they seem to understand my words. I have sworn that they will never have to suffer a bridle or saddle, for they are my dearest friends.

The horses would not make war over